The Perfect DOG

The PERFECT DOG

by

Kevin O'Malley

Dragonfly Books — New York

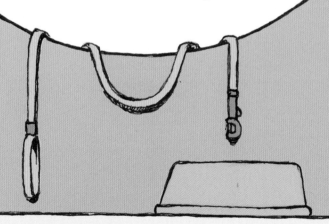

FOR DARA, WHO HAS THE PERFECT DOG

Published in the United States by Dragonfly Books, an imprint of
Random House Children's Books, a division of Penguin Random House LLC, New York.
Originally published in hardcover in the United States by
Crown Books for Young Readers, New York, in 2016.
Dragonfly Books with the colophon is a registered trademark of Penguin Random House LLC.

Visit us on the Web! rhcbooks.com
Educators and librarians, for a variety of teaching tools,
visit us at RHTeachersLibrarians.com

The Library of Congress has cataloged the hardcover edition of this work as follows:
Names: O'Malley, Kevin, 1961– author, illustrator.
Title: The perfect dog / Kevin O'Malley.
Description: First edition. | New York : Crown Books for Young Readers, [2016] | Summary:
"A girl tries to pick the perfect dog for her, but in the end, the right dog picks her"– Provided by publisher.
Identifiers: LCCN 2015029102 | ISBN 978-1-101-93441-8 (hardback) | ISBN 978-1-101-93442-5 (glb) |
ISBN 978-1-101-93443-2 (epub)
Subjects: | CYAC: Dogs–Fiction. | BISAC: JUVENILE FICTION / Animals / Dogs. |
JUVENILE FICTION / Animals / Pets. | JUVENILE FICTION / Concepts / Words.
Classification: LCC PZ7.O526 Pe 2016 | DDC [E]–dc23
ISBN 978-1-101-93444-9 (pbk.)

MANUFACTURED IN CHINA   10 9 8 7 6 5 4   First Dragonfly Books Edition
Random House Children's Books supports the
First Amendment and celebrates the right to read.

My parents said
we could get a dog.

And I know
the perfect
dog....

The perfect dog should be **big** . . .

The perfect dog
should be small . . .

smaller . . .

The perfect dog
should have
LONG
hair...

The perfect dog should **NOT** be too...

Or too . . .

The perfect dog should be *fancy* . . .

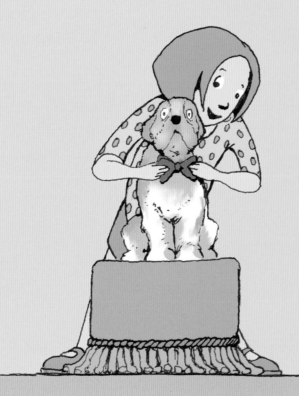

fancier...

The perfect dog should be *fast*...

The perfect dog
should be

snuggly . . .

snugglier . . .

The perfect dog should **NOT** be too...

Or too . . .

So we went to get the perfect dog.

We finally decided the perfect dog should be . . .

But then . . .

The perfect dog found me!

Chow Chow

Afghan Hound

Airedale Terrier

Bulldog

Dalmatian

Shih Tzu